COLORING BOOK WITH POSITIVITY

EVERY DAY IS A FRESH START

I am in control of my thoughts

I am grateful for all that I have

I AM SURROUNDED BY LOVE AND POSITIVITY

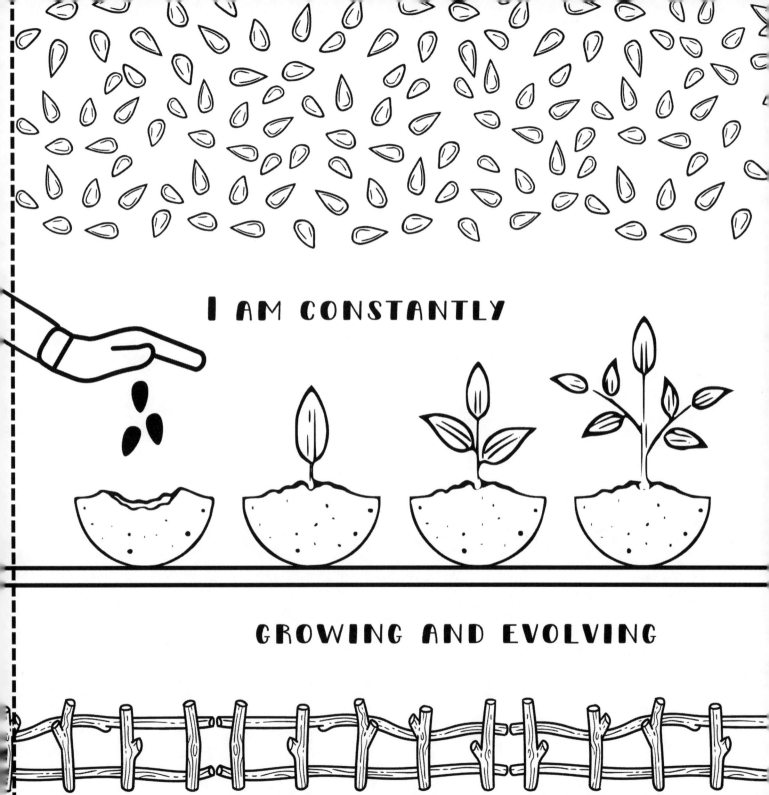

I AM CONSTANTLY

GROWING AND EVOLVING

I deserve to be
happy and fulfilled

I TRUST THE JOURNEY OF LIFE

I AM IN HARMONY WITH THE UNIVERSE.

Made in the USA
Monee, IL
01 December 2024

71834675R00031